TaleSpinners I

Lisa Eisenberg

A Pacemaker® Book

FEARON EDUCATION
a division of

PITMAN LEARNING, INC.

Belmont, California

TaleSpinners™ I

Balloon Spies
Better Than New
Death Angel
Dream Pirate
Golden God
Johnny Tall Dog
The Joker
Man in the Cage

Senior development editor: Christopher Ransom Miller
Content editor: Carol B. Whiteley
Production manager: Patricia Clappison
Design manager: Eleanor Mennick
Text designer and illustrator: Innographics
Cover designer: Bob Haydock

ISBN–0–8224–6728–3
Library of Congress Catalog Card Number:
80–65912
Printed in the United States of America.

1.9 8 7 6 5 4 3 2 1

Contents

POLICE PUZZLED BY CHRISTMAS EVE BREAK-IN

Scarsdale, NY . . . The home of millionaire Clifton Winkles was broken into and robbed last night, and up to $250,000 worth of money, silver, art, and jewels were taken. As of late this afternoon, police had few leads on the case. Captain Jay Morgan of the Scarsdale police stated, "The burglar or burglars came in through a downstairs window and cleaned the place out while the family slept. The alarm was turned off and the safe opened without any problem. Whoever took the money and jewels didn't leave any clues at all."

1

On the Subway

It was the day before New Year's Eve in New York City. Ann Iwasaki hurried along 8th Street toward the Sixth Avenue Subway. As she walked, snow fell with blizzard force. Burying her face in the top of her wool coat, she leaned into the driving wind. Then she glanced down at her watch. It was almost 9:00 A.M.

Maybe I'll be on time today, Ann thought. And maybe Mr. Peterson won't start screaming at me. Harold Peterson was the owner of Peterson's Exotic Pet Parlor where Ann had a part-time job. During the Christmas season, though, she had been working there from 9:30 to 5:00. And she had been late almost every day for the last two weeks.

As Ann reached Sixth Avenue, the cold wind hit her full in the face. She gasped for air, rounded the corner, then joined the crowd of people rushing down the steps to the subway station.

A train was just pulling in as Ann reached the platform. Pushing her way through the crowd, she stepped into the second car. Then she slid into the nearest empty seat. Just as the subway doors closed, a heavy man in an army jacket sat down next to her. He took up so much room that Ann could barely move.

Oh, well, she thought as she pressed her body toward the window. I'm lucky to have a seat at all. At least I can read.

She pulled her wet wool cap off her head and pushed her hair away from her face. Then she reached into the book bag she had put down by her feet. The first book she pulled out was *The History of American Literature*. She made a face and stuffed the book back into the bag.

I'll read that one tonight, Ann told herself, thinking guiltily of her classes at New York University. She had planned to do a lot of studying over the holidays. But so far, she hadn't been able to make herself do any at all.

At last her searching hand found the book she wanted. With a small smile, she pulled out *The Complete Sherlock Holmes* and settled back in her seat to read. She was in the middle of a story about the famous detective called "The Adventure of the Blue Carbuncle."

There were only a few pages to go, and Ann finished quickly. Smiling at the story's ending, she put down the book and looked around the subway car.

I wonder what Sherlock Holmes would see with his knowing eyes, Ann thought. I wonder if it's really possible to tell what people do for a living or where they live just by observing them. Sherlock Holmes could probably figure out where every person in this car is going. But to me they're just blank faces.

Just then, the man next to Ann reached into his pocket. He pulled out a small, flat bottle and took a quick drink from it. Then he looked over at Ann, who quickly turned her face toward the window.

Well, at least I can figure out where *he's* been, she thought. And how he's going to spend his day. His breath is enough to knock you over.

While the man took another drink, Ann picked up her book again. She began reading a new story, "The Adventure of the Speckled

Band." Soon she had forgotten all about the subway train. It was 1883, and she was helping Holmes and Watson solve a case in the streets of London.

But Ann didn't have long to read. In a few minutes, the train pulled into a station and stopped. With a groan, the man with the bottle pulled himself up and headed for the door. Ann closed her book and looked out the window. Suddenly she gasped. This was her stop. She had to get off. But before she could get up, the doors had closed and the train started to move.

Not *again,* she thought. I'll never get to the Pet Parlor by 9:30. Mr. Peterson is really going to scream at me this time.

Tapping her fingers on her seat, Ann rode to the next stop and hurried out onto the platform. There she wasted several minutes waiting for a train headed back in the other direction. At last she decided it would be faster to walk. She rushed up the stairs to the street and started to run the six blocks to the Pet Parlor.

By the time she turned the corner onto 57th Street, she was fighting for breath. Snow covered her hat and coat, and her hands and face were stiff from the cold. She made a face as she felt water coming in through the bottoms of her boots. Finally she saw the green and yellow sign that said Peterson's Exotic Pet Parlor. She was 10 minutes late, but at least she was there.

The store looked quiet. Maybe I'll get away with it today, she thought to herself. Maybe Mr. Peterson isn't here yet, and I can open up the shop myself. He'll never have to know I was late.

With that thought to drive her on, Ann ran the last few steps to the shop. She felt in her pocket for her ring of keys. But before she could find it, the pet shop door opened from the inside. Mr. Peterson walked out into the street.

Ann gave a little gasp and stepped backward. Then suddenly her boot slipped on a patch of ice and she was on the ground at Mr. Peterson's feet.

2

The Missing Keys

For a few long seconds, Ann sat on the snow-covered sidewalk looking up at her boss. Then she started to struggle to her feet. Mr. Peterson didn't make a move to help her. His cold stare reminded her of one of the South American fish in the tanks in the Pet Parlor.

"Mr. Peterson," Ann began when she was finally standing up. "I'm sorry I'm late again. I —"

"My dear Ms. Iwasaki," Mr. Peterson said in a loud, icy voice. "I'm not interested in hearing any more of your wonderful excuses for being late. I've had to listen to them almost every day for two weeks. Can you give me one good reason why I shouldn't fire you on the spot?"

Mr. Peterson's voice was so loud that he didn't hear the footsteps coming up behind him. When he was finally quiet, Ann pointed over his shoulder.

"Excuse me, Mr. Peterson," she said. "I think we have a customer."

The pet shop owner wheeled around. A woman was standing there wearing a thick fur coat and very heavy make-up. Under her right arm she held a tiny gray poodle.

Ann could almost see Mr. Peterson pulling himself together. His face went from stiff to smiling. Suddenly his voice became warm and friendly.

"Good morning, my dear lady," he said. "My, what a nice little dog! Won't you both come in out of the cold?"

Mr. Peterson reached backward and pushed open the door of the pet shop. When the woman had gone inside, he looked at Ann and his angry voice returned. "Get in there and take care of her," he snapped. "And remember to lock up when you leave tonight. We'll finish our little talk tomorrow."

Before Ann could speak, Mr. Peterson turned and headed off into the snowstorm. As she watched him go, she wondered where he went on all the days he left her alone in the Pet Parlor. Shaking her head, she hurried into the warm shop, pulled off her coat, and threw it on a chair.

The woman in the fur coat had set her poodle down on the counter. The little dog was wearing a wool cap and sweater and red rubber boots. His heavy rhinestone collar sparkled in the bright lights of the shop. As she walked to the counter, Ann thought the dog looked hot and tired.

The customer started talking at once. "This is Sweetie," she said. "I want to board him for a while. He eats lean meat only. And his coat needs to be brushed out every day. Be sure he stays warm—I don't want him to catch a cold."

"We'll take good care of him," Ann told the woman with a smile. She handed her a piece of paper. "Would you mind writing your name and address on this for our records?"

As the woman started to write, Ann reached out and took off Sweetie's cap. Then she patted the dog's warm head. He looked up at her and slowly blinked his eyes.

"Thank you, Mrs. Zane," Ann said when the woman handed back the paper. "But wait

—you've forgotten to give me your address."

"I'll be out of town. You won't be able to reach me. I'll be traveling a lot."

"Oh. Well, can you give me any idea when you'll be picking Sweetie up?"

Mrs. Zane twisted her leather gloves in her hands. "Pick him up?" she said with a nervous laugh. "Well . . . I'm not sure when I'll be back. I'll call you when I know." She bent down and kissed Sweetie on the top of his head. "You be a good little boy now," she whispered. Then she turned to leave.

But at the door she stopped. "There's one more thing, Ms. . . . Ms. . . . ."

"Iwasaki."

"Ms. Iwasaki. And it's very important. I don't want you to let anyone else collect Sweetie from this shop. I'm the only one who can pick the dog up. No matter what happens. *No one else.*"

"Of course," Ann told her, and she patted Sweetie again. His owner tossed her smooth hair, pulled her fur coat tightly about her, and slipped out into the snow.

Ann shook her head and started pulling off Sweetie's boots. "How can you stand her?" she asked the dog. "That stupid rhinestone collar is so heavy that you can hardly walk!"

With gentle fingers, Ann removed the poodle's collar and sweater. Then she wrote his name on a name tag, snapped it onto a light silver chain, and slipped it over his head. She hung the boots and collar on a hook next to some bird toys and stuffed the sweater and cap into a drawer. Finally, she carried Sweetie into the back room and put him into a cage next to a giant Doberman pinscher. The Doberman started to bark and throw himself against the sides of his cage.

"Stop it, Killer," Ann told him. "You don't have a mean bone in your body, and you know it. Besides, I don't have time for your games today. I have a lot to do, and I'm running late."

She hurried to the front of the shop. There she worked quickly to clean and feed the parrots, turtles, and other animals. When she had finished with the mice and rabbits, she sighed and looked over at Groucho, Mr. Peterson's pet monkey. His cage was on a high shelf in a front corner of the shop.

Ann hated to do anything for Groucho. Every time she went near his cage, he grabbed her hair. Once he had pulled so hard that she had to scream for Mr. Peterson's help. The monkey's thin hands were as strong as a man's.

Carefully Ann went over to Groucho's cage and peeked through the bars. The monkey's dish was half full of food, and he still had plenty of water.

"Good. I can take care of you later, Groucho," she told him, ducking away from his long fingers. She fished in her pocket and found her key ring. Then she crossed the room and unlocked the glass cases in which the snakes were kept.

Ann didn't like Groucho. But she did like the snakes. Every day she tried to spend a few minutes holding them and watching them. But today as she picked up a scarlet king snake, she heard someone come in through the door. She turned around with the black-, red-, and yellow-banded snake in her hands.

The gray-haired man in the doorway gave a high-pitched scream. "Get that thing away from me!" he yelled, backing toward the corner.

Ann took a step forward. "Don't worry," she said. "He can't hurt you."

The man's face was filled with fear. "Just put it away!" he cried. "I don't want it anywhere near me!"

Moving as quickly as she could, Ann put the snake back into its case and locked the door. But when she turned around again, she saw that the man was only inches away from Groucho's cage. The monkey had reached a long arm through the bars and was reaching frantically for the man's thick gray hair.

"Watch out behind you!" Ann yelled. The man looked quickly over his shoulder and jumped forward, just in time. Then, breathing hard, he crossed the room and leaned on the counter. As Ann observed his wild hair, small round eyes, and large hooked nose, she was reminded of the Amazon parrot whose cage she had just cleaned. Then she noticed the man's fingernails. They were so long they curled over at the tops.

How awful, she thought. They're like ugly little hooks. Or claws. He really is like a big bird.

As Ann stared, the man gave her a quick nervous smile. His teeth were yellow and small. "Sorry I got so upset," he said. "I just can't stand snakes. They scare me to death. And then that monkey. Anyway, I'm here to pick up the poodle."

"Poodle?"

"Right. You know, the little gray one. My wife brought it in this morning," the man said.

"You mean Sweetie?" Ann asked. "But he just got here. Your wife said you were going away."

The man flashed his yellow teeth at her again. "I know, I know," he said. "But we just decided we didn't want to go on vacation without him." He put a hand into his pocket. "What's the bill come to?"

"Well, I'm sorry, sir," Ann said. "I can't let anyone but Mrs. Zane pick him up. She told me to be sure that only she collected him."

The nervous little smile left the man's face. His small eyes narrowed, and he ran his clawlike nails through his thick hair. "Maybe you didn't hear what I said, sister," he snapped. "I'm *Mr.* Zane. That's *my* dog. And I'm taking him out of here. Now where is he?"

Without waiting for an answer, the man started marching around the shop and looking into cages. Just then, Killer gave a loud bark from the back room. Mr. Zane wheeled around and headed toward the sound.

Before he reached the back door, Ann stepped up to the counter. "If you go back there, I'll set off the burglar alarm," she said. "The button is right here under the counter."

Mr. Zane stopped in his tracks and turned toward Ann. She bit her lip, wondering if he had believed her lie. Mr. Peterson was far too cheap to put in a burglar alarm. He had said he'd rather let himself be robbed so he could collect the insurance money.

As Ann and Mr. Zane stared at each other, the shop door opened and three customers walked in. Saying something under his breath, Mr. Zane moved away from the back room. As Ann left the counter and went over to help the customers, she saw him open the door and go out.

Taking a deep breath, Ann asked the customers if she could help them. She showed them a few things, but soon they left without buying anything. Ann decided to finish cleaning and feeding the snakes. She went to the counter to get her key ring. But when she reached for it, it wasn't there.

I'm sure I put it here, Ann thought. What a great day this is turning out to be. Why does everything happen to me?

Ann crawled around on the floor behind the counter looking for the key ring. But she had no luck. Then she decided she must have put the keys somewhere else. She would have to go over every inch of the shop. But an hour and a half and two customers later, she gave up. The keys were not to be found.

Ann stared at the snakes' locked cases and groaned. The snakes didn't eat often, but they were supposed to be fed that day. If she couldn't open their cases, they would get awfully hungry. And she wouldn't be able to lock the shop when it was time to close up. There was only one thing to do. She would have to call Mr. Peterson. And he wasn't going to like it.

3

The Phone Call

Ann spent the next several minutes trying to track down Mr. Peterson. But she didn't have his home number, and she couldn't find any listing for him in the phone book. At last she called a restaurant where her boss often stopped for a drink. The owner promised to have Mr. Peterson call her if he came in.

For the rest of the day, Ann was alone in the shop. The snowstorm kept any customers away. Usually Ann liked being alone with the animals and birds. But today she couldn't enjoy it. The strange Mr. Zane and the loss of her keys made her feel jumpy.

At 2:00, she got out the turkey sandwich and apple she had brought from home. But after a few bites, she knew she was too nervous even to eat. So she decided to read more of "The Adventure of the Speckled Band," only to discover it was about a snake. Ann slammed the book down on the counter. Don't remind me, she thought to herself.

By 4:30, Ann was very nervous. It was almost time to leave and still no Mr. Peterson. If he doesn't get here by 5:00, she told herself, I'll break into the snakes' cases to feed them. Then I'll sleep here tonight to be sure the shop is safe.

But at 4:55, Mr. Peterson came rushing through the door. He brushed the snow off his coat and spoke in a cold voice. "The owner of the Blue Ribbon said you'd called. What's the problem now?"

Even though his greeting was cold, Ann was happy to see him. In a rush of words, she told him about the lost keys.

Mr. Peterson's eyes bulged as Ann was speaking. When she finished, the pet shop owner reached into his pocket, brought out his own keys, and slammed them down onto the counter. Then, with an angry look, he said, "Have another set of keys made tonight. Bring them in tomorrow. And get here *on time!*" He left the shop in a cold rush of wind and snow.

It took Ann almost half an hour to finish up her work for the day. Then she put on her coat and hat, went out into the street, and locked the front door.

Looking around, she saw that the snow had stopped. The air was cold and clear, so she decided to walk over to Fifth Avenue and take a bus home. The bus wasn't as fast as the subway, but she could look out at the Christmas decorations and lighted windows.

In 35 minutes, Ann climbed down from the bus in Greenwich Village. Quickly she headed toward the apartment building where she lived with her grandmother. As she walked, the cold air turned her nose red, and the hard snow crunched under her boots.

She was only a few yards from her building when she heard footsteps running down the sidewalk. Suddenly, in spite of the cold, she started to sweat. For no reason she could think of, her heart started to pound with fear, and she broke into a run.

Then she heard someone calling her. "Slow down, Ann! It's only me!"

Ann slid wildly on a patch of ice and came to a stop. As she was struggling to catch her breath, a young man in a police officer's uniform ran up and gave her a quick hug.

"Danny Takahashi!" Ann said when she was able to speak. "I shouldn't speak to you for frightening me like that. I thought I was about to be murdered!"

Danny laughed and took her arm. "A little nervous, are you?" he said. Then he walked with Ann toward the apartment building. Danny lived in a tiny one-bedroom flat two floors above Ann. They had known each other for almost five years.

"You're still shaking, Ann," Danny said in a minute. He stopped and looked at her. "What's the matter with you? I can't have scared you *that* much."

Ann smiled and shook her head. "It's nothing," she said. They walked into the building and onto the elevator. Ann pressed the button for 10, and Danny pressed 12.

Halfway up, Ann said, "I guess I'm upset because I had such an awful day. First I was late to work. Then a really terrible man came into the shop. And *then* I lost my keys. I'm almost sure Mr. Peterson is going to fire me."

"I don't understand why you want to work for him anyway. He sounds like a real jerk."

"I guess he thinks *I'm* a real jerk!"

"Well, even if you've had a bad day, don't tell your grandmother about it. Remember what the doctor said about her heart. She's not supposed to worry about anything."

"I know," said Ann. "But worrying is what she does best."

In a few seconds, the elevator reached the 10th floor, and Ann stepped out into the hall. Danny stood between the elevator doors to keep them open.

"Are you still going out on the town with me tomorrow night?" he asked.

"Well, I don't know. I have so much studying to do. I only have a week to finish my American literature paper."

Danny's mouth dropped open. "You can't study on New Year's Eve!" he cried.

He looked so upset that Ann started to laugh. "I guess you're right," she said. "OK. I'll see you tomorrow night."

"Great!" said Danny, backing into the elevator. "And before we go out, I want you to stop in at my apartment. I still haven't given you your Christmas present."

Ann was still smiling as she entered Apartment 10–A. She walked straight into the cheerful yellow kitchen and saw her grandmother bending over the stove. The little woman came over and gave Ann a kiss. She barely came up to Ann's shoulder.

"Hi, Ba-chan!" Ann said. "What's for dinner?"

Before her grandmother could answer, the telephone started to ring in the living room. Ann sighed and went to get it. She pulled off her coat and dropped it on a chair by the Christmas tree. Then she picked up the phone.

"Hello?" she said.

"Is this Ms. Iwasaki from the pet shop?" a woman's voice asked.

Ann was sure she had heard the voice before. But she couldn't remember where.

"This is Ms. Iwasaki," she answered. "Who's this?"

"Mrs. Zane. You remember, I brought my poodle Sweetie into your shop this morning. I told you I'd call when I wanted to pick him up."

Ann rolled her eyes. Why is this crazy woman calling me at home? she thought.

"Well," Mrs. Zane was saying. "I changed my mind about boarding the dog. I want to pick him up now."

"*Now?*" Ann asked.

"Well, yes. Can you meet me at the shop?"

Ann began to feel angry. "I'm afraid not, Mrs. Zane," she said. "The shop is closed."

Mrs. Zane sounded very upset. "I have to get Sweetie back," she said. "Right away. It's a matter of life and death."

Now I've heard everything, Ann thought. "Listen, Mrs. Zane," she said into the phone. "I'll meet you at the shop first thing tomorrow morning. Not tonight. I'll try to get there early. Is 9:15 all right?"

Mrs. Zane didn't speak for a moment. But Ann could hear her breathing on the other end of the line. "Is 9:15 all right, Mrs. Zane?" she asked again.

A gentle click sounded in Ann's ear. Then the phone went dead.

4

Killer's Cage

Ann put down the phone with a shake of her head and stared into the bright lights on the Christmas tree. She saw the reflection of her troubled face in the shining red and green decorations. I wonder if I should have told Mrs. Zane about her husband's visit to the pet shop, she thought.

"Time to eat, Annie," her grandmother called, coming into the living room. "Who was that on the phone?"

"A customer from the pet shop," Ann told her. "I wonder how she got my home phone number."

Ba-chan shook her head and hurried back into the kitchen. "I think you should stop working at that place," she said. "You worry about it all the time. You should be thinking about your studies instead."

Ann smiled and followed her grandmother to the round wooden table where they ate. "I know you're right, Ba-chan," she said. "But it's odd. This woman—Mrs. Zane—sounded really upset. Over a *poodle*. And then she hung up so suddenly. It was almost as if — "

"Forget that silly shop and eat your dinner, Annie! You're getting too thin."

Ann sighed and looked down at her full plate. I wonder if Ba-chan will ever stop treating me as if I was three years old, she thought. Then, all at once, she realized that she hadn't had any food since breakfast. Everything smelled wonderful. To her grandmother's delight, she quickly cleaned her plate and asked for a second helping.

After dinner, Ann washed the dishes and watched the news on television. Then she carried her book bag into her bedroom and shut the door. For the next four hours, she worked on her American Literature paper.

At 11:30, she set her alarm and climbed into bed with her Sherlock Holmes book. In a short time, she finished "The Adventure of the Speckled Band." Then she started reading "The Adventure of the Engineer's Thumb." By the time she put down the book and turned off the light, it was past 1:00 A.M.

What would Holmes have thought of Mr. and Mrs. Zane? she asked herself. With a yawn, she pulled up the covers. She tried to think of everything she had observed about the strange couple. But all she could remember were Mr. Zane's awful fingernails. In a few minutes, she was fast asleep.

When the alarm went off the next morning, Ann leaped out of bed. She ran to the bathroom and grabbed her toothbrush. As she looked at her face in the mirror, she thought how surprised Mr. Peterson would be when she showed up early at the Pet Parlor. "If you really hurry," she told her reflection, "you might even beat him there."

She ran a brush through her hair and went back into the bedroom. There she pulled on a gray wool skirt and a blue turtleneck. Without making her bed, she rushed out to the living room and began to struggle into her boots. Her grandmother came out of the kitchen and gave her a cold stare. "No breakfast again, I suppose?"

"I'll eat something on the way, Ba-chan," Ann lied. She jumped up and gave the tiny woman a quick kiss. Then, with her coat over her shoulder, she hurried out of the apartment and caught the elevator on its way down.

By the time Ann left the subway at 57th Street, it was only 8:45. From half a block away, Ann could see that the shades were still down in the windows of the Pet Parlor. Mr. Peterson hadn't come in yet. Ann grinned.

Running the last few steps to the shop, she reached into her coat pocket and pulled out her keys. Then she gasped. The keys in her hand were Mr. Peterson's—not hers. She had forgotten to have another set made!

Maybe I can still get them before Mr. Peterson shows up, Ann thought quickly. She looked up and down the street. But since it was only 8:45, nothing was open yet.

All at once, Mr. Peterson's bulging eyes and red face flashed into Ann's mind. She leaned with a sigh against the pet shop door and looked up at the clear winter sky. Suddenly she realized she was falling backward, and she jumped forward to stay on her feet. Looking at the door, Ann saw that it had come open when she had leaned on it. Not only hadn't it been locked, it hadn't even been tightly closed.

Ann bit her lip and thought back to the day before. Can I be going out of my mind? she asked herself. I'm *sure* I locked that door last night.

Fearing what she might find, she stepped into the shop and pulled up the shades. Usually, when the light came into the store in the morning, the birds woke up and started to whistle and call. But today they sat quietly in their cages and stared at each other.

Ann let out a long sigh as she looked around. Nothing seemed out of place. It doesn't look like anyone was here, she told herself. For once I was lucky. She started to take off her coat.

All at once, a horrible screaming laugh came from the corner behind her. Ann dropped her book bag and wheeled around. Groucho grabbed the bars of his cage and laughed again. Then he kicked his tin water dish as hard as he could. It sailed out of the cage and crashed to the floor.

"Stop it, you stupid monkey," Ann snapped at him. "I wish someone would break in here and steal *you!* You scared me to death!"

As she spoke, Ann heard a sound in another part of the shop. She turned toward the noise. In the corner, the giant black Doberman lay, rolled into a tight ball.

"Killer!" Ann said. "How did you get out of your cage?"

The big dog sank lower, trying to hide his face under his front legs. One frightened eye looked out at Ann as he gave a low growl. That was when Ann looked away from Killer and across the floor—to the trail of dark, wet footprints that led to the back room.

"What have you gotten into?" she asked the Doberman. "You've tracked something all over the place!"

She started toward the back of the shop and whistled for the dog to follow. He gave another low growl and stayed where he was. With a sigh, Ann pulled open the door and went into the back alone.

The room was very dark. Even when Ann's fingers felt along the wall and pressed the lightswitch, it stayed dark. The lights didn't work. Shaking her head, Ann started across the room to the side window. "Ouch!" she cried. She had crashed into a large box in the middle of the floor. "What is that doing there?"

Bending down to rub her leg with her left hand, she reached with her right and pulled the string on the window shade next to her. The shade rolled up with a loud snap, and the morning light spilled into the room.

Ann let out a groan as she looked around. It seemed as if everything in the room had been tossed into the air and dropped. Cans of dog food had rolled into every corner, and several large bags of dry meal had been torn open and spilled out. A broken dog cage sat against the wall as if it had been thrown there. The overhead light had been smashed, and dangerous pieces of sharp glass were everywhere. And in the center of the floor was a wide circle of thick, dark liquid.

Slowly Ann stepped over some cans of dog food and moved toward the dark pool. As she walked, a little dachshund named Frank started barking at her. The rest of the dogs were very quiet.

Suddenly Ann caught her breath and stood very still. In front of her was Killer's cage, just beyond the dark liquid on the floor. Its door was tightly closed and locked. And though Killer was still out in the front room, something else was in his cage.

Ann came a few steps closer to the cage and bent over to look in. Was it what she thought it was? It was. She jumped backward, tripped over a dog dish, and went down hard on her hands and knees. Now she was even closer to the man who was twisted up inside Killer's cage. He was staring out at her. But he wasn't seeing her. Ann looked at his wide, blank stare and quiet face. She knew the man was dead.

5

The Professor

By 9:15, Peterson's Exotic Pet Parlor was filled with police. Ann sat on a chair behind the counter, quietly watching a tank of goldfish. Killer rested on the floor beside her, his body pressed up against her leg. Since she had rushed out of the back room a short while ago, the Doberman hadn't left her side.

At 9:45, after she had answered several questions, Ann looked out of the pet store window. Mr. Peterson was coming toward the shop. He stared at the police cars in the street, then hurried in the door.

"Ms. Iwasaki," he began. "What's going —"

At that moment, two men wheeled a stretcher out of the back room. As he saw the shape of a person's body under the white sheet, Mr. Peterson stopped speaking. His mouth dropped open.

Just then Danny Takahashi rushed through the door. His nose was red, and his eyes were watering as if he'd been running through the cold air. They searched the front room. "Ann," he called when he saw her. "I was down at the station when you telephoned in. I heard your name. Are you all right? What happened? Did somebody bump off that jerk Peterson?"

At the sound of his name, Mr. Peterson turned and gave Danny his most bulging stare. Then he walked into the back room and asked a police officer what was going on.

In a shaking voice, Ann told her friend what had happened. "I feel terrible about it, Danny," she ended. "Somehow, I feel I should have known something like this was going to happen."

"You couldn't have. You're probably just upset because you can't be sure you locked up last night."

Ann twisted her hands together on her lap. "That's the one thing I *am* sure of," she said quietly. "I've gone over it again and again in my mind. I know I locked that door."

"OK, OK, I believe you. It probably wouldn't have made any difference anyway.

I'm sure the killer would have found a way to get in, locked door or not. But listen, you're probably tired from all this. And I have to get back to work. Let me drop you off at your apartment on my way to the station."

A white-haired police captain named Hazelrigg had heard Ann and Danny talking. "Not just yet," he said to Ann. "We have a few more questions to ask you. I'll see that you get home later."

"OK," Danny said to Ann. "Looks like you've got to stay. I'll call you at home in a while."

When Danny was gone, the captain dragged another chair behind the counter and sat down. He looked at Killer curled up at Ann's feet.

"Nice dog," he said to Ann. "What's his name?"

"Killer," Ann told him. At the same time, Killer looked at Captain Hazelrigg and growled.

"Oh," the police officer said, pushing his chair a few feet away and laughing nervously. Then he said, "I have just a few more questions for you, Ms. Iwasaki. May I call you Ann while we talk?"

"OK," Ann told him.

"Fine," he answered. "Now, you've already told me that you've never seen the man in the cage before. Are you still sure about that?"

"Yes, of course. Have you found out anything about him?"

"Well, we think so, but nothing's sure. He doesn't have an ID on him, so we don't know where he lives. We did find a pair of glasses in his pocket, though. The name on the case is Marcus Zane."

Ann felt hot blood rush to her face. "No!" she said. "That's not him!"

The police captain gave her a hard stare. "You just told me you didn't know the man."

"That's right, I don't know *him*. But Mr. Zane was in here yesterday. And he didn't look anything like the person in the cage. He had gray hair and little eyes and long fingernails like *claws*."

Captain Hazelrigg let out a long breath and closed his eyes. "Tell me everything you can remember about the day before," he told her. And when Ann had finished, he asked her to go over her story again. She had the feeling he didn't believe a word she was saying.

At last the captain told her to walk around the shop to see if anything had been taken. As he followed her into the back room, they could hear Mr. Peterson's high, angry voice.

"I don't understand this at all!" he was saying. "Why would a stranger come into my shop, have a fight, murder another stranger, and leave without even stealing anything? Why, I have parrots out there worth hundreds of dollars! And there's always money in the cash drawer. It just doesn't make sense."

As Ann looked around the torn-up room, she had to laugh at Mr. Peterson's words. All she could think of was a burglar trying to sneak out of the shop with a screaming parrot under a coat. Then something snapped in her brain. "Oh!" she said out loud. "Something *is* missing."

Everyone in the room turned to stare at her.

"It's Sweetie," Ann went on in a rush. "I didn't notice until now. But Sweetie isn't here."

"Sweetie?" Mr. Peterson squeaked. "Who is Sweetie?"

Then everyone started talking at once. Finally Captain Hazelrigg took Ann aside so he could hear her answers to his questions. They went on for a few more hours. Finally, in the middle of the afternoon, the police captain told Ann he was ready to drive her home.

Captain Hazelrigg fought his way through the heavy traffic on Seventh Avenue, his mind lost in thought. Once Ann asked him a question, but he didn't seem to hear her. She didn't try to talk to him again.

It was half an hour before the captain pulled up in front of Ann's building in Greenwich Village. Then he asked suddenly, "How long have you been working for this guy Peterson?"

Ann turned to look at him in surprise. "Mr. Peterson? I've worked for him part-time for about two months. Why?"

"You ever notice anything odd about him? Any strange people coming and going in the shop?"

Ann laughed out loud. "There are *lots* of strange people coming and going in that shop," she said. Then she was silent for a few seconds. "I do wonder, though, where Mr. Peterson goes during the day sometimes," she said in a more serious voice.

Captain Hazelrigg just nodded. Then he said, "Ann, I'm sure you've told me everything you can think of that might help in solving the murder. But in cases like this, people often forget little things that later turn out to be important. If you remember anything else you saw or heard, please call me right away."

"Sure, Captain," Ann said and climbed out of the car. But the captain called after her.

"There's one more thing. Don't forget that we're dealing with a dangerous killer here. It looks like he—or she—or they—are after something, and they may not stop until they get it."

Ann nodded, waved good-bye, and walked slowly into the building. As she rode up on the elevator, she thought about the day she had just been through. Then she thought about her grandmother. What am I going to tell Ba-chan? she wondered. She could have a heart attack if she hears about the murder at the pet shop. It's a good thing she never reads the newspaper!

When Ann entered the apartment, her tiny grandmother looked up in surprise. "You're home early, Annie," she said. "If I'd known you were going to be here so soon, I'd have asked him to wait."

"Asked who to wait?"

"One of your professors from the university. He was just here."

"Professor?"

"*Yes*, Annie," said her grandmother. "I asked him what he taught, and he said American literature. He was a little odd looking, I thought. But so nice. We had tea. He seemed to be very interested in you. He wanted to know when you'd be home, but I said I couldn't be sure. So he said to tell you he'd see you later."

All at once, Ba-chan stopped talking and gave her granddaughter a sharp look. "Annie, what's wrong?" she asked. "You look strange. Are you sick? Is that why you're home early?"

"Ba-chan . . . ," Ann began. Her voice cracked and she stopped.

"What *is* it, Annie?"

"Ba-chan, the man who was here wasn't who he said he was. My American literature professor is a woman."

6

Danny's Gift

Ba-chan put her hands on her hips and shook her head. "He wasn't your American literature professor?" she said. "Well, maybe I got it wrong. Maybe he teaches a different subject."

Ann looked at her grandmother. She was sure no professor from the university would come to her home. But it was very possible that the man who had come had something to do with the murder. Ann decided not to upset her grandmother with any possible trouble, though. Ba-chan could worry herself into a heart attack. And she would try to keep me under lock and key if she thought I might be in any danger, Ann thought.

"He was probably my German professor," Ann said to her grandmother with a smile.

But as Ba-chan walked out of the room, Ann pictured her German professor's wheelchair and long white beard. Ba-chan would certainly have noticed them. She hoped her grandmother would never run into the man.

As Ann stood thinking, her grandmother was already banging pots and pans around on the stove. But Ann wasn't ready to eat.

"Don't make anything for me, Ba-chan," she called. "I really don't feel very well. I think I'll go lie down." Maybe in her quiet room, with the door closed, she would have a chance to think. She needed time to figure out who Ba-chan's strange visitor might have been. And what ought to be done about him.

But Ba-chan wouldn't leave Ann alone. She rushed over and put her small hand on Ann's face. "You don't feel hot. But you could be coming down with a cold. Sleep is the best thing. You get right into bed, and I'll make you some tea with honey."

Ann rolled her eyes and turned toward her room. She pulled off her clothes and climbed into bed. Seconds later, Ba-chan hurried in with a pile of extra blankets. Then she ran out and came back with a hot water bottle. In a minute or two, she was back again with the tea.

The fourth time her grandmother came into her room, Ann quickly closed her eyes and started snoring. Ba-chan tiptoed away.

"At last," Ann sighed to herself. "Now who was this strange 'professor' who came to see me. What did he want?" She knew she should call Captain Hazelrigg to report the visitor. But the phone was in the living room, and she didn't want Ba-chan to hear her. Besides, the man could just have been selling magazines and got her name from a list.

Leaning back on her pillow, Ann wondered why Captain Hazelrigg had been so interested in her boss. She smiled at the idea of Mr. Peterson being a dangerous criminal. Maybe the Pet Parlor is just a front, she thought. And Mr. Peterson is the leader of a band of bank robbers.

With a soft laugh, she rolled over onto her stomach and asked herself what Sherlock Holmes would do with this case. She tried to remember something Holmes had told Watson in "A Study in Scarlet." It had to do with thinking backward. When he was dealing with an *effect,* Holmes said, he always reasoned backward to figure out the *cause.*

Ann rolled over again and turned on a little yellow lamp next to the bed. She got up and crossed the room to her desk. When she had found a pen and a pad of paper, she crawled back under the blankets. Then she wrote the words *cause* and *effect* at the top of the first page and drew a long line between them. Under *effect* she wrote, "A dead man is discovered at the Pet Parlor."

Ann leaned back. "So far so good," she whispered to herself. "Now why did he go there? Was he meeting someone? Or was he looking for something? And if he was looking for something, what was it?"

Just then she heard the telephone ring. Ba-chan's light footsteps hurried to get it.

Oh, no, Ann thought. It's probably Captain Hazelrigg, and he'll tell her the whole story. She threw down the pen and paper and quickly pulled on her robe. Then she went out to the living room.

When Ba-chan saw her, she put a hand over the telephone. "You get back in bed right now, Annie!" she said.

"Who is it?"

"It's Danny. I was just telling him you're too sick to go out tonight."

Ann thought fast. She had forgotten about the date in all the excitement. But maybe it would be a good idea to go—and have Ba-chan go with them. It would get the two women out of the apartment in case the "professor" decided to come back that night and turned out to be dangerous.

"All of a sudden I feel a lot better," Ann said out loud. "I think I will go out with Danny. And you can come with us!"

Ba-chan's mouth became a firm line. "You aren't going anywhere tonight," she said. "And neither am I."

The look on her grandmother's face told Ann there was no point in starting a fight. "OK, Ba-chan. We won't go out. But let's at least go up to Danny's apartment for a while. We can watch the crowd in Times Square on television. You know how you like to see the ball drop at midnight."

Ba-chan looked hard at Ann's hopeful face. "Oh, all right," she said, turning back to the telephone. "But only because it's New Year's Eve."

Later that night, Ann and Ba-chan were sitting in front of Danny's giant color television watching the people in Times Square. Danny was running around the apartment, opening bags of potato chips and pouring drinks. At last he ducked into his bedroom and came back out with a small red and gold package.

"Merry Christmas, Ann," he said. "And Happy New Year." He leaned over and kissed her on the top of her head. Then he backed away and winked at Ba-chan.

"Oh, thank you, Danny," Ann said. "I wish I had something for you. But I sent away for your present in the mail, and it still hasn't come yet, and — "

"I know, I know. You told me all that. Now open it."

Ba-chan was leaning forward in her chair. "Hurry up, Annie!" she said. "What could it be?"

Quickly Ann tore away the gold ribbon and red paper. Then she looked down at the small black box in her hands. The name of one of New York's most expensive jewelry stores was printed on the top.

"Danny," she began slowly. "You shouldn't have. . . ."

"Come on," Danny broke in. "I had fun buying it. And besides, it didn't cost that much."

Ann smiled at him and slowly opened the box. Then her eyes grew wide. Inside the box was a long, thin silver chain. Hanging from the center of the chain was a tiny, shining diamond.

"Do you like it?" Danny asked at once. "It's the real thing. I know it's small, but —"

"It's beautiful!" Ann said. "Just beautiful."

"Take it out of the box, Annie," Ba-chan said. "Hold it so I can see it better."

Carefully Ann lifted the thin chain from the box and held it out in front of her. The little diamond started to swing back and forth, sparkling in the light of the room.

Suddenly Ann could hear Sherlock Holmes speaking to Watson in "A Study in Scarlet." A person's brain is like a "little empty attic," the great detective had said. And only the most important ideas and observations should be allowed to enter it. Something about the necklace was inviting an important thought to enter Ann's "empty attic." She closed her eyes and tried to pin it down.

Ba-chan wasn't sitting quietly, though. She was grinning from ear to ear. "It's so pretty, Danny!" she cried. "It will look beautiful with Ann's blue dress. Then she turned to her granddaughter. "Try it on, Annie. Let me look at it on you."

But Ann wasn't listening. She was staring straight ahead at the shining circle of silver hanging in her hand. Her mind was racing, and her heart was beating wildly. She was almost sure she'd figured out what had happened at the Pet Parlor. And why a man had been killed.

7

Followed

The clock on the wall above Danny's television said 11:00. Ann wondered if Captain Hazelrigg was still on duty, and how she could call him without Ba-chan's hearing her.

Suddenly she thought of something. She jumped to her feet and smiled at her grandmother. "I've got a great idea," she said. "Why don't you hold the necklace while I run downstairs and get into my blue dress? Then I'll come back up and try on the diamond."

Danny and Ba-chan both looked delighted, so Ann hurried out the door and down the stairs. As soon as she entered her own apartment, she raced to the living room and called Captain Hazelrigg. Her heart sank when a strange man answered and told her the captain wasn't there.

"Is there any message, miss?" the cheerful voice asked.

"Well . . . I guess so. This is Ann Iwasaki. The captain told me to call him if I remembered anything new about the pet shop case. I have thought of one thing, and I think it might be important. Of course, it could be nothing too. Anyway, I really need to talk to the captain about it."

"OK, miss. I'll have Captain Hazelrigg get in touch with you as soon as possible."

Ann hung up the phone and started pacing back and forth in front of the Christmas tree. After 10 minutes, the captain still hadn't called back. Ann made a quick decision. She would go to the Pet Parlor and see herself if what she thought was true. Marching into the bedroom, she pulled on a pair of jeans and a thick sweater. She was halfway out of the apartment door when she remembered Danny and Ba-chan waiting upstairs.

Quickly she walked back into the living room and called Danny's number. "Something important has come up," she said when her friend answered. "I have to go to the Pet

Parlor. Please tell Ba-chan I went to bed. And keep her in your apartment till midnight."

Before Danny had a chance to speak, Ann hung up. Then she ran out to the hall to catch the elevator. If I take a taxicab, she told herself on the ride down, I should be able to get to 57th Street and back by 12:00.

When Ann stepped out of the building, she saw right away that a cab was out of the question. She had forgotten that it was New Year's Eve. Every taxi that passed was either off duty or filled with cheering people in party hats. She decided then to take the subway. With hurried steps, she crossed Fifth Avenue and turned west on 9th Street.

As Ann walked, she took short, quick breaths of the icy winter air. Inside her gloves, her fingers were already growing cold. She dug her hands into her coat pockets and tried to move faster. To her surprise, she saw that very few people were out in the street.

They're all inside where it's warm, she thought. Welcoming the New Year. I must be crazy to be out now. But she kept on walking.

About halfway between Fifth and Sixth Avenues, Ann heard the sound of footsteps on the sidewalk behind her. At least I'm not the only one outside tonight, she told herself. She looked over her shoulder, but there was no one else on the street. With a sigh, she ducked her head against the wind and moved on. Then all at once, she heard footsteps behind her again.

Suddenly Ann's stomach turned over. Her heart jumped wildly. Was she making it up, or were the footsteps picking up speed?

Take it easy, she told herself. Those footsteps are probably on their way to a party. Anyway, all you have to do is make it to the corner. There are always lots of people on Sixth Avenue.

Skirting a dangerous patch of ice, Ann half-ran the remaining distance to the end of the block. But as she rounded the corner, she groaned out loud. The usually busy street was empty of both cars and people. The only sound was the wind howling its icy song.

Ann stopped running and leaned against the side of a dime-store building. Her chest hurt from the cold air, and her breath came in loud gasps. Just 30 seconds' rest is all you get, she told herself, and she closed her eyes a few moments. Then she stepped away from the store and looked back around the corner. Once again 9th Street appeared to be empty.

What a wonderful detective *I* am, Ann thought as she headed toward the subway station. I'm afraid of everything that moves. What would Sherlock Holmes say?

At the corner of 8th Street, the wind blew so hard that Ann had trouble walking. She pulled up the collar of her coat and fished in her pocket for a subway token. Then, taking a deep breath, she forced herself over to the stairs that led to the trains.

With a last look over her shoulder, Ann started down. When she reached the platform, she was happy to see a few other people waiting there. She bought a newspaper from a machine and leaned against a pole while she read the front page.

In a few minutes' time, the light from a subway train appeared in the darkness. The hot wind blew Ann's hair out around her face. When the train came to a stop, Ann placed her newspaper under her arm. Climbing on board, she sat down in a seat near the back of the last car.

There were three other people riding in the car. One was a bearded man who sat at the front with a brown paper bag in his hand. He was leaning sideways in his seat and appeared to be sound asleep. Sitting across from Ann were a friendly looking older man and woman. But as the train came to a stop at 23rd Street, the woman turned to the man and pulled at his jacket. The two riders stood up and stepped off the train.

Ann watched the older couple start across the platform. They saw her looking at them and gave her a little wave. For some reason, Ann had the wild idea of leaping up and running after them. She fought it off, holding the side of the seat to keep herself in it.

Stop being so nervous, she told herself. No one is following you. She picked up her paper and forced herself to read a story about a football player. Suddenly she heard a loud sigh from the front of the car. She glanced up and saw the bearded man fall over and slide onto the floor.

He's probably just had too much to drink, she thought, and looked back at her paper. Then she remembered all the stories she had heard about New Yorkers never helping each other out. Putting down her paper, she got to her feet and walked up to where the man lay.

When she bent down to see his face, the man opened his eyes and grinned at her. "Happy New Year!" he said in a thick voice. Then he sat up and tried to hug her.

Ann made a face and moved quickly back. But as she was about to return to her seat, she saw something out of the corner of her eye.

In the connecting space between the last two subway cars, the tall figure of a man stood pressed against the windowed door. It was too dark to see the man's face, but Ann felt sure that he was watching her. And as she stared at him, the handle on the door slowly started to turn.

CHAPTER

8

Alone in a Crowd

For a few long seconds, Ann stood still in terror. Then she felt something brush against her leg. It was the man on the floor, trying to pull himself up. With a last look at the turning handle, Ann wheeled around and rushed toward the back of the car.

Please hurry, she willed the speeding train. Hurry and get to the next stop.

Luck was with her. As she silently made her wish, she saw station lights up ahead and felt the train slowing down. The doors opened, and Ann leaped out onto the platform. From the corner of her eye, she saw the flash of a red-checked jacket coming through the connecting door. The bearded man now stood in the middle of the car singing "Auld

Lang Syne." Ann raced up the stairs that led to the outside.

When she came out onto 42nd Street, she stopped to figure out where she was. She stood staring at her frightened reflection in the glass windows of Number Two Times Square. If I go west, I'm likely to run into a police officer, she thought to herself. She turned and started running. After half a block, she glanced over her shoulder. A hundred yards back, the light of a street lamp showed a splash of red color moving quickly up the street.

Suddenly Ann could hear people. Lots of them. She ran toward the sound, and in seconds people were all around her. She felt herself being swept along in the edge of a giant crowd out into the street. For a moment, she didn't know what was happening. Then she realized she was in the middle of Times Square, where thousands of New Yorkers were waiting for midnight and the new year.

Frantically Ann struggled to see over the heads of the laughing, singing people. Was someone pushing toward her through the crowd? Someone in a red-checked jacket?

"Please," Ann yelled, turning to the man next to her. "Please help me. I'm being followed."

"What's that, kid?" the man shouted back at her.

"I'm being *followed!*" Ann screamed. But the man had already been carried away by the crowd.

Now Ann wheeled around and grabbed the arm of a woman in a bright green coat. Once again, she tried to get help. But it was impossible to make her voice heard over the noise.

The woman didn't know what Ann was saying. "Happy New Year, doll!" she yelled. Then she too was swept away.

Ann grew more frightened as she felt herself being pushed deeper and deeper into the center of the square. Then she had a thought. Maybe I'm really safe here. Maybe it's better here than by myself on the street. What could happen in the middle of this crowd?

Just then a loud bang sounded in her left ear. Someone had exploded a firecracker. Bang! The sound came again, and everyone in the street laughed and cheered. Suddenly the crowd didn't seem that inviting. Ann bit back a wild scream.

I could be shot to death right here, she told herself with a sinking feeling. And no one would ever notice. I've got to get out of this crowd and find a police officer.

Lowering her head, she started to force her way through the crowd. Slowly she struggled across the street toward the sidewalk. When she reached it, she took a short step up and crashed against something cold and hard. It was a snow-covered garbage can sitting by the curb.

"Excuse me," she said to a man standing near the can. He was wearing a high fur hat and laughing with a friend. Ann put a hand on the man's shoulder and pushed herself up onto the can. At last she could see out over the crowd.

There was no sign of the running figure in the red-checked coat. But about half a block to the north, Ann could see a mounted police officer on a tired-looking black horse.

Maybe he can help me get out of here, Ann thought. And get me back home. Or maybe he even has a radio! He could get in touch with Captain Hazelrigg. I must have been crazy to leave home and not just wait for his call.

As Ann climbed down from the garbage can, she saw an open stretch of sidewalk on her right. Pushing her way through the people around her, she hurried across the open area in the direction of the police officer. As she ran, she heard the sound of a man's voice behind her. "Excuse me," he was saying loudly again and again. "Excuse me. Let me through."

Oh, no, Ann said to herself. She glanced back and saw the awful red checks only a few yards away. As she looked back, she crashed into someone in front of her. It was the bearded man from the subway. "Happy New Year, honey," he said in a tired voice, and tried to hug her again. But Ann pushed him away and started running in and out among the people along the street.

As she ran, she listened for the sound of footsteps behind her. It was impossible to hear anything except shouts and cheers. Soon, as her hair and face became wet, she realized that another snowstorm had begun. Before long she could barely see where she was running.

All at once, Ann felt her foot slip over the edge of the curb. She had to grab a pole to keep from falling. At least I made it to the corner, she thought. Fighting for breath, she stood very still and peered through the heavy snow. The police officer was gone.

He's got to be here somewhere, Ann thought. She looked harder into the crowd. Then she heard a noise she hadn't heard before. It was the whinny of a horse.

Ann breathed a long sigh and started walking in the direction of the sound. At last the large shape of a horse and rider appeared before her. She broke into a run. "Officer!" she called. "Help!"

Suddenly a hand came down hard on her shoulder and jerked her to a stop, snapping her neck backward. Ann felt her blood turn to ice. Then, as she looked down at the hand that held her, she gasped. The nails at the ends of the bony fingers were so long they curled over at the top. Like claws.

CHAPTER

9

Claws

As Ann stared, the clawlike fingers left her shoulder and moved to circle the back of her neck. Just then, the mounted police officer rode over. His sad-looking horse breathed hot air in Ann's face.

"Did I hear you calling me, miss? What's the trouble?"

Ann started to speak, but the hand on her neck got much tighter. It was a clear warning.

"I . . . there's nothing wrong, officer," Ann said at last. "My—ah—friend and I thought we were lost. But we're not."

The officer gave her a tired look and shook his head. Then he moved off into the snowstorm. Ann twisted around so she could see the small eyes and large hooked nose of the man who held her.

"Mr. Zane," she began. Then she stopped —she had remembered the real Marcus Zane. "But you're *not* Mr. Zane. He . . ."

The man flashed his yellow teeth at her. "No, I'm *not* Mr. Zane. Marcus Zane was a stupid, foolish pig. And we both know what happened to *him*."

Ann thought of the bloody body in Killer's cage and swallowed hard. "But who are you?"

The man's long, cold fingers moved up and down Ann's neck as he spoke, the nails rubbing lightly over her skin. "People call me Claws," the man said with a laugh. "Now let's get going."

"Where? What do you want with me?"

"Don't get smart, sister," Claws told her. "You know what I want. And you're going to take me up to the pet shop and hand it over."

Claws pushed Ann in the direction of the nearest subway. He held her arm tightly as he dragged her down the steps. In the station, he fished two tokens out of his pocket and put them in the machine. When a train pulled into the station, he put his arm around Ann in a friendly way. Then smiling, he pulled her through the doors and down onto a seat.

After the train had started, Claws swept the snow from his red-checked jacket, pulled out a little white brush, and began shining his terrible nails. Once he glanced up at Ann and grinned.

"There's one thing I don't understand, sister," he said. "How did you know the diamonds on the poodle's collar were real?"

So I was right! Ann thought. Trying to keep her face smooth, she said, "I don't know what you're talking about."

"Oh, come off it. You spotted the diamonds and took the collar off the dog. Then you must have put it somewhere in the shop. Now you're waiting to slip the jewels out one day after work."

Ann's throat was so dry she could barely swallow. "How do you know the collar is still in the shop? Maybe I already took it somewhere else."

"Nice try," Claws laughed. "But I've been keeping an eye on you for two days. You didn't go anywhere but your apartment. And I've *been* there already. I checked your room while the old lady made tea."

My fake "professor," Ann thought. I should have known it was him. How could I be so stupid?

The train was slowing down to pull into a station. It was the 57th Street station—the stop for Peterson's Exotic Pet Parlor. Ann glanced at Claws. He was still bent over, hard at work on his nails. She saw one small chance, but she knew she had to take it.

As the doors to the train slid open, Ann leaped to her feet as fast as she could. She threw herself off the train, crashing into a candy machine as she went. She was halfway up the stairs to the street when a long arm grabbed her from behind and jerked her to a stop.

"We'll walk the rest of the way," Claws said in a hard voice. "You try that again, and you'll be sorry. Collar or no collar."

The gray-haired man put his arm around Ann's shoulders once more. Then he led her up the last of the stairs and out into the driving snow. Neither of them spoke as they quickly walked the six blocks to the pet shop. Every time someone passed them on the sidewalk, Claws pushed his left hand into his pocket and gave Ann a warning hug.

When they reached the Pet Parlor, they stopped outside and waited for a group of people to go by. Then Claws twisted Ann around to face him.

"Unlock the door," he snapped.

"There's probably a police guard," Ann began. Then she broke off and bit her lip. Great, she thought to herself. Now if there *is* a police guard, I've warned him.

"Good thinking, sister," Claws said with a grin. "Maybe I'll make you my partner next time around. Now open the door—quietly."

After Ann had turned the shop key in the lock, Claws pushed the door open. Then, with one hand around her neck and the other holding a small gun, he stepped into the Pet Parlor.

The front room was filled with the peaceful sound of soft snoring. In the gentle green light of the fish tanks, Ann could see a man sleeping in a chair near the counter. She could almost reach out and touch him.

Moving quickly, Claws stepped toward the man, raised an arm, and brought it down hard. With a loud crunch, his gun slammed into the sleeping man's head. The officer let out a soft groan, slipped off his chair, and fell to the floor. He didn't move again.

Ann felt as if she might be sick. She leaned sideways against a shelf and closed her eyes. Her legs seemed very weak.

But Claws wouldn't let her be. He started shaking her so hard her head banged against the wall behind her. "Don't fall apart on me now, sister," he said. "I don't have time to waste. Get me that collar!"

Ann looked up at the man's little eyes and felt a sudden, cold anger sweep over her. She knew that if she gave him the collar, her life would be worth nothing. Even if she didn't end up stuffed into a cage like Marcus Zane.

All at once, she couldn't stand the feel of the clawlike fingers digging into her shoulder. With a quick move, she jerked her body sideways and pushed out with both hands. Claws reached out to grab her again, but she ducked away and raced around a shelf full of parrot-training books. She passed the fish and quickly snapped off their tank lights. In seconds the shop was in darkness.

"It won't work, sister," Claws said. "Just turn on the lights and I won't hurt you." He started toward her and walked straight into the bookshelf. It crashed over, cracking the corner of the glass counter.

Without a sound, Ann got down on her hands and knees and started crawling. As she moved along the counter, she felt the key ring she still held tightly in her fingers.

"Observe the small facts," Sherlock Holmes had told Watson in "The Sign of Four." And *remember* them, Ann added to herself. If only he doesn't see me, I might make it. There's a good chance he won't turn on the big lights, because someone outside would notice.

Finally she reached the end of the counter and sat up on her knees. With shaking fingers, she searched through the keys on her ring. As quietly as she could, she rose to her feet and ran her hands along the back wall.

"Ouch!" screamed Claws across the room, smashing into the sharp side of a rabbit cage. Then there was a soft pop. The gentle green lights in the fish tanks went back on one by one.

Ann could see Claws's wild gray hair standing out around his head and the black shape of his raised gun. "OK, you," he said to her. "Now tell me where that collar is. Or I'll come over there and make you tell me!"

As he spoke, Ann's searching hands finally found what they wanted. She was in a dark corner and was sure Claws couldn't tell what she was doing. She turned a key and silently pushed open a glass door. Then she reached forward and touched the cool, smooth skin of the scarlet king snake. Slowly she picked it up and pulled it out of its case.

10

Backed into a Corner

The snake felt like a piece of thick rope in Ann's hands. Quietly she stepped out into the soft light with it.

"Don't make a move, sister," Claws barked.

Ann took another step forward. "I'm holding a snake, Claws."

The man with the gun drew in a sharp breath. "That's impossible," he began. "How could you. . . ?"

Ann moved into the center of the room and held the king snake high above her head. Claws gasped and backed along the row of fish tanks. "Don't come any closer with that thing," he said. "Keep back or you're dead." His words were tough but his voice was shaking.

"Go ahead and shoot," Ann told him. "As soon as you point the gun, I'll throw this snake right at your face. It loves to wrap its body around a person's neck." She forced herself to take another step.

Claws groaned and moved toward the front corner. Then he turned to face Ann. "Listen, sister," he said with a flash of his yellow teeth. "Maybe we could work something out."

All at once, the man stopped talking. He gave a terrible yell and seemed to be falling backward. "Let go of me!" he cried, pawing frantically at the air.

Ann couldn't tell what was happening. Still holding the snake in both hands, she peered through the darkness. Had someone been hiding in the corner behind Claws?

Ann soon found out. Suddenly the shop was filled with the sound of a high, screaming laugh. Walking slowly toward the front, Ann could see two thin brown hands sticking out of a cage. They were tearing at Claws's thick gray hair. The more the killer yelled, the more the monkey laughed and pulled.

Groucho! Ann thought. I'll never complain about you again. Now just hold onto that hair until I get out of here.

Moving quickly, she placed the snake on the counter and started for the door. Crack! Claws's gun went off in his hand. With a loud smash, the bullet shattered an empty fish tank. Tiny pieces of flying glass shot into the air.

Crack! The gun fired again. Ann felt a sharp, burning pain in her shoulder, and she reached up to touch it. Her fingers felt something wet and warm. Then the walls of the pet shop started to spin around and around.

Claws was still yelling and shooting wildly as Ann slipped down to the floor. Groucho's high-pitched laugh rang in her ears. Far away, Ann thought she heard someone out in the street calling her name. Then the door of the shop banged open, and Claws's gun exploded one more time. Everything went black.

The next morning when Ann opened her eyes, she found herself staring up at Ba-chan's worried face. But the worry turned to a smile when Ba-chan saw Ann looking at her.

"So you're awake, Annie," she said. "Happy New Year's Day."

Ann tried to sit up, but Ba-chan put out a tiny hand and gently pushed her down. "You're in the hospital and need to rest," she said. "You're very lucky to be alive. Let me tell you, when I heard what you'd been up to, without a *word* to me, why I — "

A man's voice broke in on Ba-chan's speech. "Take it easy, Mrs. Iwasaki. She's been through a lot. You can yell at her tomorrow."

Ba-chan turned to look at Captain Hazelrigg, who had come up next to Ann's bed. He grinned at Ann. "You *are* lucky to be alive," he told her. "Claws Gorman is a dangerous man—with a long police record."

"Tell me everything that happened," Ann said. "I guess I passed out in the pet shop."

"Well, it seems you figured out the most important part of this case before I did. I wasted most of my time running around after your boss, Mr. Peterson. But he turned out to be clean."

"Did you find out where he goes every day?"

"Well, he spends most of his time going to kennels and other places that sell animals.

The rest of the time he walks around handing out leaflets about the Pet Parlor. You know, stuffing them under doors and sticking them onto car windows."

Ann smiled at the idea of Mr. Peterson running around in parking lots. But Captain Hazelrigg was telling her more.

"Anyway," he was saying, "last night we finally tracked down the apartment where the real Marcus Zane had been living. When we got there, we found his wife—the one who had brought Sweetie to the shop—tied up in a chair. She was more than happy to talk. It seems that she and her husband had pulled off a big robbery, along with Claws Gorman. Then Mrs. Zane had decided to take the diamonds from the job for herself."

"And she had them put onto her poodle's collar," Ann broke in. "She thought they would be safe at the Pet Parlor until she could make plans to get away. Then she would pick up Sweetie and leave town."

"Right," Captain Hazelrigg said. "But her husband heard her on the phone making travel plans and later talking with you. He figured out what she'd done, so he tied her up.

Later that night he went to break into the store and get the jewels for himself. But when he got there, he found Claws opening the front door—with your keys! Somehow Gorman got on to Mrs. Zane's plan right away. There was a fight, and Claws shot Zane and stuffed him into Killer's cage."

"And then Claws must have taken Sweetie. He didn't realize the dog wasn't wearing the collar any longer. When he did, he thought I had taken the diamonds for myself. And he came after me."

"Right again," Captain Hazelrigg said. "Claws wanted us to arrest *you!*"

Ann shook her head. "I thought the jewels on that collar were rhinestones. I only took it off Sweetie's neck because it was so heavy. Later, when my friend Danny gave me a diamond necklace, it made me think of Sweetie's jeweled collar. I remembered that Sherlock Holmes had said that the two most important things in detective work are observation and *deduction*. That means using what you've observed to figure out what you don't know. So I reasoned that the collar was the one new thing in the Pet Parlor that could have been causing all of the trouble."

Captain Hazelrigg nodded. "We found the collar last night. It was covered with diamonds taken in a Scarsdale robbery. We didn't find it before because we didn't know what we were looking for."

Ann thought of another question. "How did you know to come after me at the pet shop last night?"

"You told your friend Danny. He called me and left a message. Then he rushed up to the shop by himself. One of Claws's bullets caught him in the leg as he broke in."

Ann jerked up in the bed.

"Don't worry," the captain said. "He'll be okay. I got to the shop right after he did and had him taken to the hospital. Claws gave himself up—probably to get away from that crazy monkey."

Ann laughed. "I'll have to give Groucho some extra bananas tomorrow."

"Not tomorrow," Captain Hazelrigg said. "There's something I haven't told you. Mr. Peterson was so upset when he heard you'd almost been killed that he's giving you two weeks off. *With* pay."

"He *must* have been upset!" Ba-chan said in a dry voice. Then she pulled at Captain Hazelrigg's arm. "Let's leave so Annie can get some rest."

"Captain," Ann called as she raised herself on one elbow. "There's one more thing. What happened to Sweetie?"

Captain Hazelrigg smiled. "We picked him up at Gorman's place. Since Mrs. Zane will be in jail for a long time, Sweetie is back at the pet shop."

"Good," said Ann. "Tell Mr. Peterson Sweetie eats only lean meat and his coat needs to be brushed out every day."

Then all three of them had a good laugh.

As the two visitors went out the door, Ann lay back on the bed and closed her eyes. Smiling, she imagined herself telling Sherlock Holmes all about "The Adventure of the Poodle's Collar." Seconds later, she was fast asleep.